The Moon's Lullaby

by Josephine Nobisso

pictures by Glo Coalson

Orchard Books   New York

...olastic Inc.

Library of Congress Cataloging-in-Publication Data
Nobisso, Josephine.
The moon's lullaby / by Josephine Nobisso ; with pictures by Glo Coalson.
   p. cm.
Summary: As night settles in, a baby's yawn travels around the world, inducing sleepiness everywhere.
ISBN 0-439-29312-X (alk. paper)
[1. Yawning—Fiction. 2. Sleep—Fiction.] I. Coalson, Glo, ill. II. Title.
PZ7.N6645 Moo 2001 [E]—dc21 00-39953

10 9 8 7 6 5 4 3 2 1   01 02 03 04 05

Printed in Mexico 49

First edition, October 2001

Book design by Mina Greenstein
The text of this book is set in Perpetua bold.
The illustrations are watercolor and pastel.

Per Maria: *Che bambola!*—J.N.

For Dr. Kathryn Kimbrough Waldrep.
You mean so much to so many.—G.C.

$\mathcal{B}$y the light of the moon, the first yawn of the night began as yawns often do, with a baby's tiny mouth wrapped around it.

The baby's mother caught the yawn and let it out on a sleepy sigh. *"Yaw-awn,"* she murmured, settling down to nurse with the baby.

Their big dog skidded through the house trying to outrun the yawn, but just as he slipped outside, it walloped him on the back of the head. He stretched his great neck and lifted his broad muzzle to howl at the moon. A yapping *"YAW-AWN!"* leaped out instead.

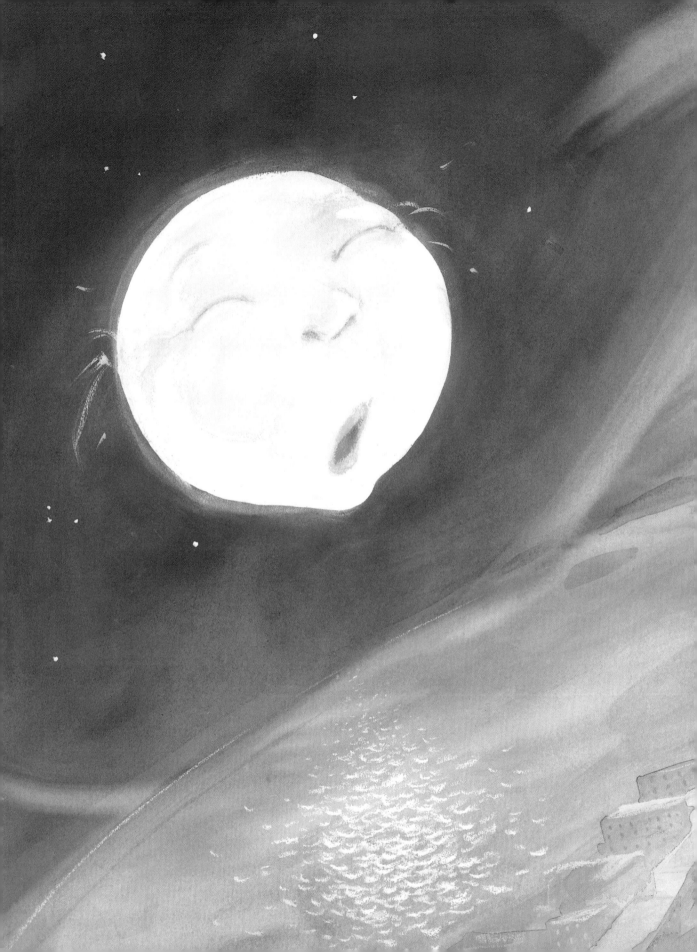

The moon blinked as the dog's yawn hit like stardust in her eye. As she made her way over the earth, her cheeks bunched up, her eyes watered over, and her nostrils twitched and flared.

"YAW-AWWWWWNNN!" she finally bellowed, over the courtyard of an adobe house. Abuelo felt the irresistible urge come over him. "Yaw-awn," he breathed. "Now say your prayers, mis hijos."

The earth spun beneath the moon, and the land dropped away. Now the moon shimmered over the ripples of a great ocean. *"YAW-AWN!"* she vibrated over the sea's great depths, flooding its waters with sleep.

A tired boy on a ship squeezed shut his burning eyes. "I'm sure I saw two black—*yaw-awn*—heads in the water!" he insisted to his aunt.

"Let's go below," she answered. "I'm sure there's—*yaw-awn*—nothing there."

A mother and baby seal who'd been playing in the ship's wake surfaced. They dived and then shot north, silent and swift, like darting shadows. When the pup poked his head through a hole in the ice, he saw that they'd come up near the igloo of a hunting family. He turned to warn his mother, snapping out a *yaw-awn* as they slithered back into the sea.

"What was that?" the family asked one another.

"Just the—*yaw-awn*—ice creaking," the grandmother told them, leading the crawl into their beds under the moonlit ice.

The earth slowly whirled beneath the moon until a mountaintop spun up. Children from an orphanage piled onto sleds, but the littlest had been left inside with a cold. Her eyes grew salty from staring at moonbeams through paper windows. She slid a window open. "Someone come keep me—*yaw-awn*—company!" she called. She smiled when the others trudged up the stairs, yawning as they kicked off straw boots.

A koala mother awoke for the night. She rustled the eucalyptus tree, searching out the tenderest leaves. As she and the moon caught sight of each other, the koala stopped munching to gather breath for a yawn. Her baby poked his head out from her pouch. They cocked their heads at each other and blinked. *"Yaw-awn,"* the baby squeaked, slipping back into his mother's pouch, all fragrant and warm.

"Look, Baba, the moon is yawning," a child pointed out from a crowded street.

Baba felt his mouth go dry as he glanced at the moon's face. "Time to—*yaw-awn*—dream, little ones," he whispered to his children. One by one, they toppled beside him on their sidewalk mat, making a pillow of their hands. *"Yaw-awn."*

A Masai boy standing guard over his herd on a windy evening leaned on his staff. As he glanced up into the sky, he gasped, overcome by the power of the moon. Stretching in delicious calm, he murmured a *yaw-awn* into a whirl of wind.

Hot-air balloonists cut across the sky, racing on the gusting wind. They reached a craggy harbor where a lone bagpiper played a welcome from atop a cliff.

"Give us a—*yaw-awn*—lullaby," they called from their baskets.

The bagpiper was surprised when his next note sounded—*YAW-AWN*—into the moonlit night.

The moon continued in her orbit, and when she shone over a tiny baby under an awning in the desert, she couldn't help beaming out one more *"Yaw-awwnnn."* So that, far from the first big city, on the other side of the world, another yawn began as yawns so often do . . .

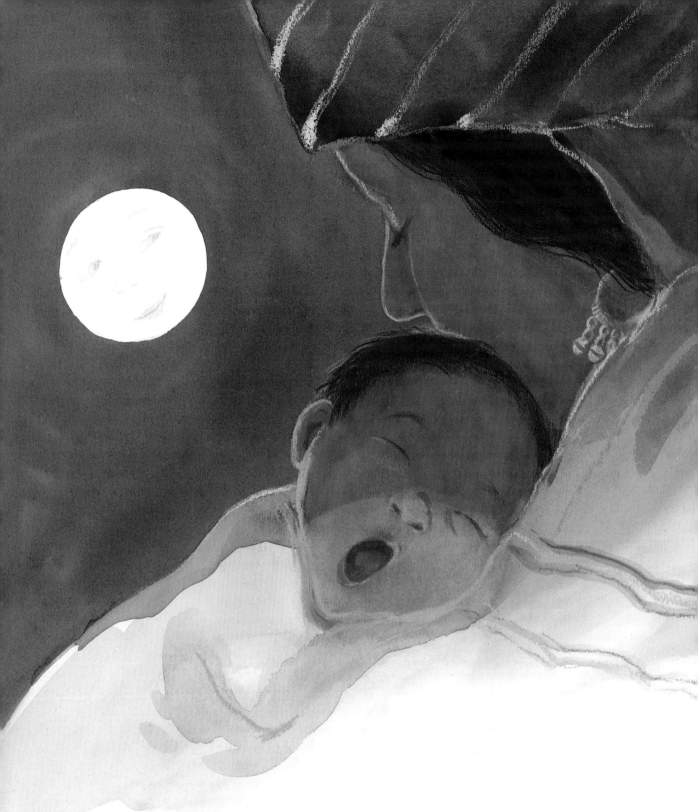

with a baby's tiny mouth wrapped around it.
"Yaw-awn."